GOLD!

DAVID SHANNON

Viking

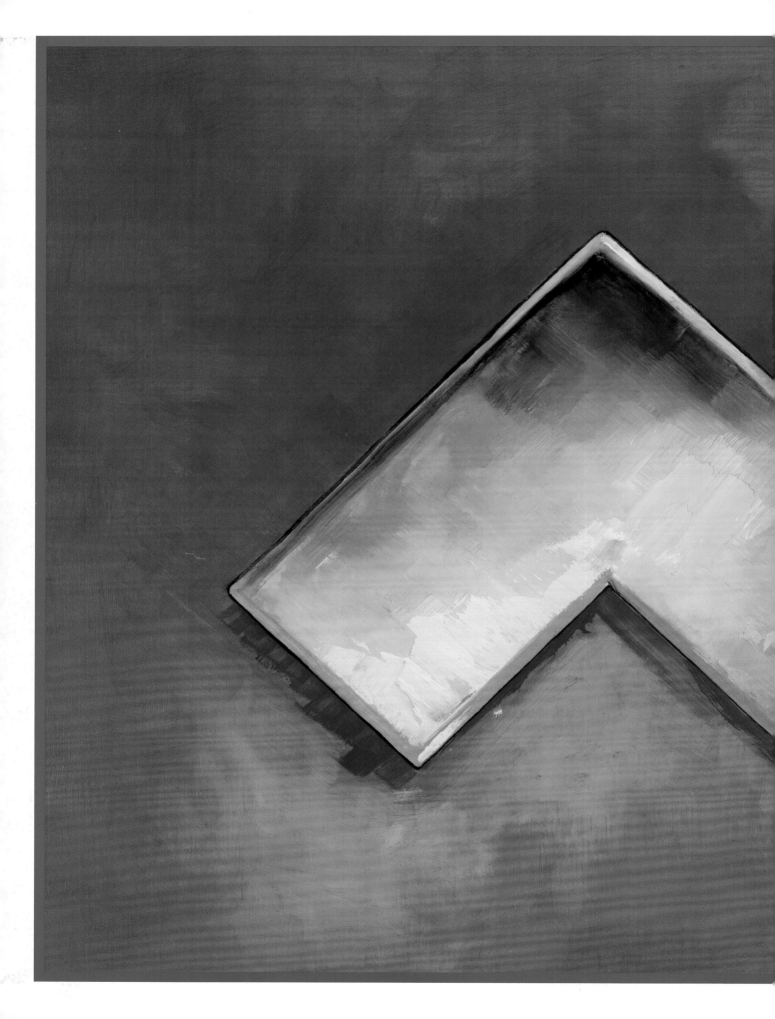

aximilian Midas

Was a peculiar little boy.
He didn't much like chocolate
And he didn't play with toys.

The first word that he uttered
When he was one year old
Wasn't *Mama,* wasn't *Papa,*

What Maxie said was *Gold!*

His parents tried to raise him right.
They said, "Be kind, not cruel."

But Max's brain got stuck on *gold*
When they taught the Golden Rule.

His mother hugged him every night.
His father read him stories.
"A hug's a hug." Maxie shrugged.
"And all those books are boring!"

He didn't like to go to school.
He cheated on his tests

And counted up his golden stars.

(There were fifty, more or less.)

But Maximilian had the touch
For raking in the dough.
He didn't think of Bad or Good,

He thought of Bought and Sold.

He started selling lemonade
Out on the parking strip,
And on the hottest, driest days,
He sold it by the sip.

He made enough to buy a house,
'Twas money quite well-spent.
But when his parents moved inside,

He charged them monthly rent.

When Sadie opened up a stand
To help some needy kids,
He dropped a mouse in her lemonade,
Then ran away and hid.

Max took over Sadie's stand,
But he had bigger plans,
And soon his lemonade was sold
In stores throughout the land.

His lemonade made millions
More than twenty banks could hold.
He never gave a cent away.
He spent it all on gold.

Statues, clocks, and
coins and bowls,
If it was made of gold,
He simply couldn't get enough—
That was how he rolled.

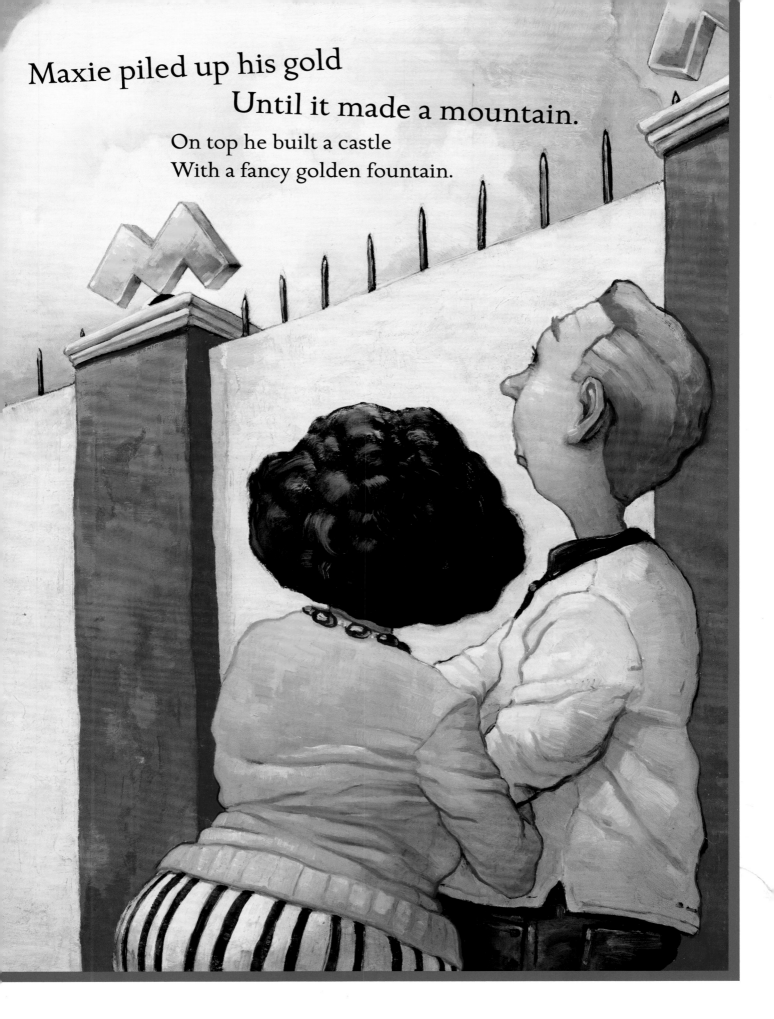

Maxie piled up his gold
                Until it made a mountain.
On top he built a castle
With a fancy golden fountain.

His furniture and walls were gold,
To Max it looked like heaven.
A lot of people said, "Not bad!
(For a kid who's only seven.)"

As time went by, Max stayed inside
And all alone got older.
His outlook didn't change a bit.
In fact,
it just got *golder*.

"Gold is what I love the most!"
Max would often cry.
"I love it more than teddy bears
Or Mother's apple pie!"

"I wish the world was made of gold,
And gold was everywhere.
I'd like to eat and drink it,
And breathe it in like air!"

That got Max to thinking
As he was making breakfast.
He came up with an idea that
Was positively reckless.

Max grabbed a bag of gold dust,
And, oh, for goodness' sakes,
He spooned it up like sugar
And dumped it on his flakes.

Maximilian took a bite.
It made his tummy tingle.
But when he chewed,
   it didn't crunch.
Instead it sort of jingled.

He suddenly felt funny,
Like his blood
      was getting cold.
He walked up to
   the window,

Then Max . . .

turned into gold!

Max was like a statue.
He couldn't move his arms.
He couldn't even walk or talk
Or set off the alarms.

Max began to panic.
He thought, *How can this be?*
No one ever comes up here.
Who's going to rescue me?!

At the bottom of the mountain,
He saw his mom and dad.
They were talking to their neighbors,
And he suddenly felt sad.

He thought about the many hugs

He'd traded for his gold,

And all the bedtime stories
That never would be told.

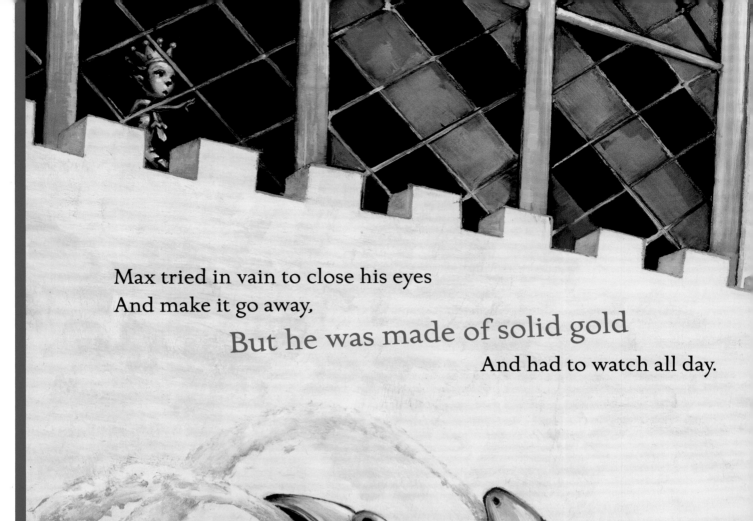

Max tried in vain to close his eyes
And make it go away,
But he was made of solid gold
And had to watch all day.

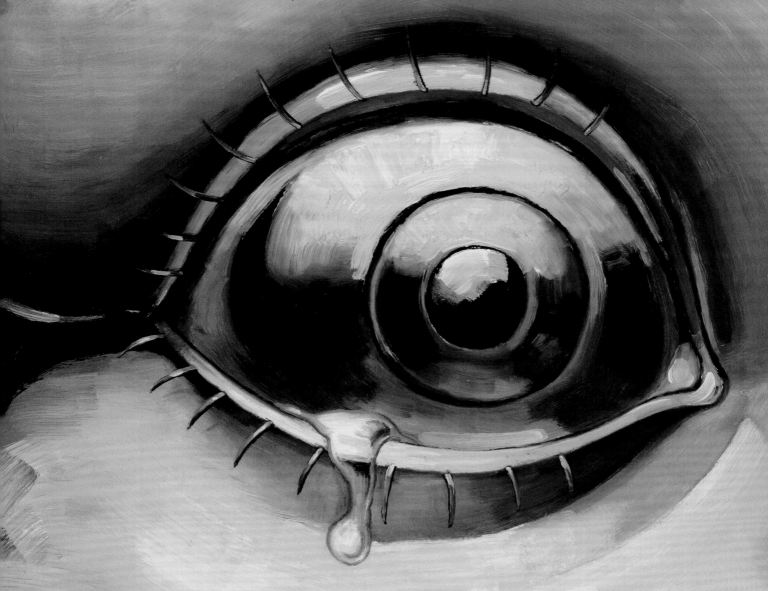

There was one thing deep inside him
That hadn't turned to gold:
A little tear that Max had saved
Since he was one year old.

And now that he was facing
A future cold and bleak,
That little tear was free at last
And rolling down his cheek.

And as it spread across his face,
What happened next was weird:
Max changed back to normal,
And his mountain disappeared!

Every bit of gold was gone,
And Max was in midair.
He landed with a *thud* and saw
His parents standing there.

"I'm sorry, Mom and Dad!"
he cried.

"My gold
was just a lie!"

His mother hugged him
twice and said,
"I'm going to bake a pie!"

His father hugged him, too, and said,
"That reminds me of a story!"
And Maxie hung on every word.
(So what if it was boring?)

They asked the neighbors over,
And Max made lemonade.

He gave them each a tall, cool glass
To sip on in the shade.

"My gold is gone,"
Max told the crowd,
"But please don't think
    I'm poor.
I've made millions
    from my lemonade,
And I'll make
    millions more!"

He apologized to Sadie,
The plucky neighbor girl,
"Will you help me
use my millions
To make
a better world?"

Then Maximilian Midas thought,
As he finished off his slice,
Gold can never make you feel . . .

As good as being nice.

THE END

For my sister, Dr. Kimmie, with love

VIKING
An imprint of Penguin Random House LLC, New York

First published in the United States of America by Viking, an imprint of Penguin Random House LLC, 2022

Visit us online at penguinrandomhouse.com.

Library of Congress Cataloging-in-Publication Data is available.

Printed in Italy

ISBN 9780593352274

1   3   5   7   9   10   8   6   4   2

LEGO

Design by Kate Renner
Text set in Golden Cockerel ITC

The artwork in this book was done in oil paint on hot-press illustration board.